THE ANCIENT EGYPTIANS

This book has been designed to bring
Egyptian history to life. The story and pictures
provide children with a useful insight into
the period. However, this is not intended
to be a history text book.

The story and pictures in this book are
all original and have been specially
commissioned for Tesco.

Published by
Tesco Stores Limited
Created by Brilliant Books Ltd
84-86 Regent Street
London W1R 5PA

First published 2000

Printed by Printer Trento S.r.l., Italy
Reproduction by Graphic Ideas Studios, England

THE ANCIENT EGYPTIANS

Illustrated by *Andy Hammond*

It was a boiling hot day and Alfie decided to go into the shed at the bottom of the garden and cool off. The door creaked open and Alfie was greeted by the familiar dank, musty smell of all the old junk in there. He often lost track of time when he was in the shed. He never quite knew what might happen while he was sorting through the curious collection of things…

Under a tatty rug, Alfie found a desk.
He put his hand deep into one of the
dusty drawers and felt something cold.
He pulled it out and saw that it was a slab
of stone with lots of squiggles and little
drawings on it.

"It looks ancient," thought Alfie.
"I wonder what it is?" He rubbed the stone
to try and get some of the dust and cobwebs
off it and suddenly he felt a shudder go right
through him. Alfie recognised the strange
tingling feeling and shut his eyes tight – he
was going on one of his adventures!

Alfie found himself standing in a market.
There were men selling bread, animals,
cloth, fruit and vegetables, big clay
pots and some beautiful vases.

Alfie watched as one old man swapped a sack of flour for four chickens, and two other men traded a gold bracelet for a big heap of cloth and some beautiful beads. No one had any money and although the system of bartering, or swapping, seemed to work quite well, there was a lot of arguing!

There was also a large man walking round with a fierce-looking baboon on a lead. It kept sniffing the things that people were carrying — to make sure there weren't any stolen goods inside!

"Where on earth am I?" wondered Alfie.
People were dressed very simply, but everything
seemed very well organised. He walked round the
corner of a squat-looking house and stopped dead
in his tracks! Straight ahead of him was the largest
river he had ever seen. It was very beautiful. But
standing next to it was something even more
amazing. Quite near the riverbank were
three enormous pyramids that stood
glinting in the hot sun. Alfie recognised
them immediately – the Great Pyramids!
He was in Ancient Egypt!

Alfie started walking towards the river.
"So this is what the River Nile looks like,"
thought Alfie. He stood and watched as
several little boats slowly sailed past him.
He was just wondering how close
he would be able to get to
the Great Pyramid,
when he heard a
faint sobbing sound
coming from a small
clump of palm trees.

Right in the middle of the trees was
a man holding his head in his hands,
weeping. Tears were streaming down
his face. "What's the matter?" asked Alfie.
"I'm a coward," wailed the man, "but I'm
going to die tomorrow and I don't want to!"
"You look all right to me," said Alfie,
trying to sound as cheerful as possible.

"You don't understand," snivelled the man, "I'm fine, but the Pharaoh, our ruler, is going to die tomorrow. It says so in the stars!"

"Oh!" said Alfie. "But why does that mean you should die as well?"

"I am his astrologer. And when the Pharaoh dies all his servants will be killed too, so we can carry on helping him in his afterlife!"

Alfie was amazed. It seemed awful that perfectly healthy people were going to be killed just because of some funny Ancient Egyptian superstition.

"How do you know the Pharaoh is going to die tomorrow?" he asked.

"It's in the stars – they never lie!" the man wailed.

"Oh, I see," said Alfie, not at all sure that he did.

"You mustn't die!" said Alfie.
"You should just hide for a while."
Alfie decided he had to help the man work
out an escape plan. But as he sat down,
something sharp dug into him. It was the old
bit of stone. Alfie took it out of his tunic.
The man, whose name was Nefret, picked it up.
"This is amazing!" he said, looking at Alfie
curiously. "It seems to give directions to a
secret tomb in the Great Pyramid!"
"Perhaps you could hide there!" said Alfie.

After Alfie and Nefret had made their plans, they waited for it to get dark. Little boats sailed up and down the Nile. Eventually there was a beautiful sunset, then at last it was time to go.

By the time Alfie and Nefret reached the foot of the Pyramids, the first stars were already twinkling above them. Nefret looked up nervously. "The great god Re will punish me for hiding!" moaned the poor man.

"I'm sure he won't," said Alfie.

Suddenly, they heard shouts. Some guards had spotted Nefret's torch!

"Quick!" said Nefret. "The entrance will be guarded, but if your stone is right, there's another way in! Follow me!"

Alfie and Nefret
scrambled up the side
of the pyramid, but the voices
behind them were getting
nearer! At last Nefret said,
"I think this should be it". He pushed
on one side of a great block of stone and
to Alfie's amazement the whole thing began to
swivel! There before them was a narrow tunnel!

Alfie wasn't
at all sure that he wanted to
go into it, but he didn't like the
sound of the guards who were chasing
them either. The tunnel was very dark and
Nefret's flickering torch made lots of scary
shadows. They crawled along the tunnel for ages.
Alfie was just thinking how sore his knees were
getting when he suddenly heard echoing voices –
ahead of them. Nefret put out his torch and Alfie
couldn't see a thing. He stretched out to touch
Nefret, but there was no one there!

"Psst!" Alfie looked up and could just make out Nefret waving at him. There was another tunnel sloping upwards. Alfie scrambled after him. Eventually Nefret lit his torch again and they saw a big door with lots more drawings and squiggles on it.

Echoing whispers were coming from the tunnel. Nefret and Alfie pushed and pushed but the door wouldn't budge. The whispers were getting nearer! In desperation, Nefret looked at Alfie's stone again and pushed one of the stones beside the door. And as if by magic the big door slid open!

Alfie peered inside. "Wow!" said Alfie
(rather loudly). His eyes grew bigger
and bigger. It was the secret tomb!
There, right in front of him, was a huge
chest full of sparkling jewels and gold!
And lying in the middle of the tomb was
a great big coffin! Nefret and Alfie crept
up to it, they held their breath
and peered inside.

There, was a beautiful blue and gold casket.
Nefret gently lifted the lid ... and
lying underneath was a mummy – wrapped
from head to foot in bandages.
At that moment, they heard loud whispers
right outside the tomb! Nefret quickly blew
out his lamp and, before Alfie had a chance to
stop him, Nefret picked him up and popped
him into the coffin! He landed right on
top of the funny-smelling mummy...
and screamed!

Suddenly the tomb was filled with light.
"What have we here?" rumbled a nasty deep voice.
Three ugly faces were looking down at Alfie.
One of the men was holding a large bronze knife!
"There's enough treasure in here for us all to be
rich for life," said the ugliest of the three men.
"But we can't have anyone knowing we were here.
Kill the boy!" he hissed. Alfie saw the bronze
knife being raised above him and shut his eyes...

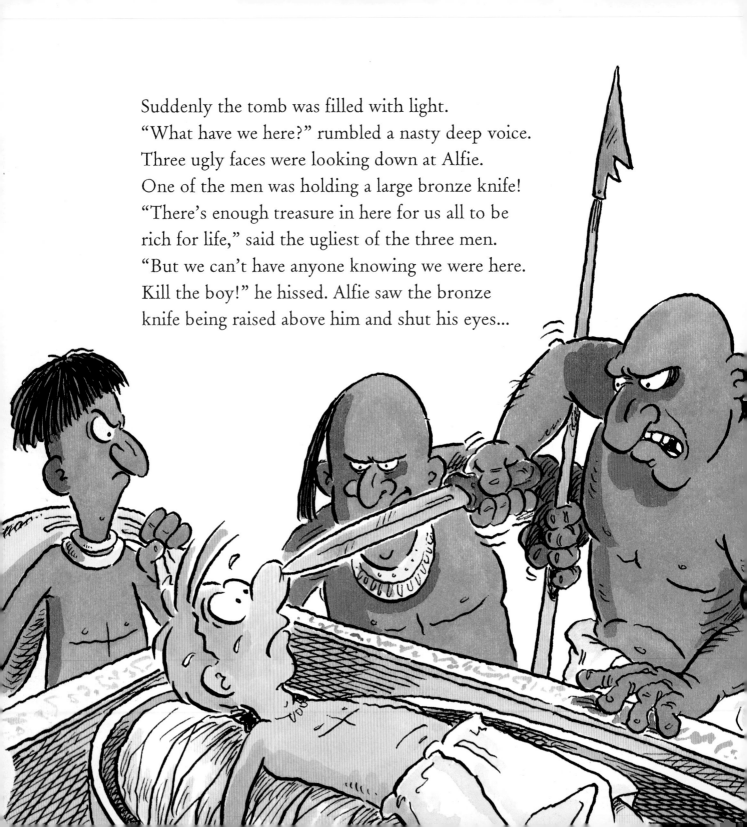

"Stop! Stop!" cried Nefret, who had leapt out of the shadows. "There are guards searching for us in the pyramid! If you don't want to get caught, you should leave now!"

"Nice try!" snarled the leader.

The villain let out a very unpleasant laugh, then stopped abruptly. In the distance there was the unmistakable sound of more voices – the guards were on their way to the tomb.

"Quick! Get the treasure! Get the treasure!" yelled the chief thief. The grave robbers stuffed as much of the treasure as they could into sacks. They were so greedy that they left it too late. The guards came running round the door!

There was a terrible struggle, but at last the guards managed to pin the thieves against the wall.

"You got here in the nick of time!" said Alfie, to the head guard, climbing out of the coffin. "They were going to kill me and steal all the treasure! But Nefret stopped them!"

The head guard seemed very impressed. "It seems you have been very brave!" he said, smiling at Nefret. "You risked your life following these scoundrels into the pyramid." Nefret blinked and looked rather embarrassed, but the guard continued, "I'm sure the Pharaoh will want to thank you in person."

The next morning, Nefret was miserable.
He'd been told that the Pharaoh only had hours
to live and Nefret knew exactly what that meant!
Nefret and Alfie were taken to a big room in
the Pharaoh's palace. Lying on a huge pile of
cushions was the most powerful man in the world!
"Ah Nefret," said the Pharaoh in a weak, croaky
voice, "I gather that you saved my grandfather's
tomb from being robbed. I am very ill, and I will
soon be dead, but I have decided to spare you so
that you may guard my own tomb."
"Oh thank you! Thank you!" cried Nefret.
"I will never forget your kindness!"
The Pharaoh smiled at Alfie and
then shut his eyes.

Outside the palace, Nefret waved goodbye to Alfie, then he ran off to tell his family the wonderful news. Alfie slumped down against a tree. He'd been up all night. He was exhausted!

He must have nodded off, because the next thing he knew he was back in the old garden shed. He stood up and shook his head to clear it. There was no sign of the stone with squiggles on it – maybe it had all been a dream? But then why were his knees so sore? He pulled up his trousers to have a look at them, and there on his leg was a bit of very, very old-looking bandage!